D0875728

The Wind off the Small Isles

Also by Mary Stewart

Madam, Will You Talk?
Wildfire at Midnight
Thunder on the Right
Nine Coaches Waiting
My Brother Michael
The Ivy Tree
The Moon-Spinners
This Rough Magic
Airs Above the Ground
The Gabriel Hounds
Touch Not the Cat
Thornyhold
Stormy Petrel
Rose Cottage

THE MERLIN SERIES

The Crystal Cave
The Hollow Hills
The Last Enchantment
The Wicked Day
The Prince and the Pilgrim

MARY STEWART

The Wind off the Small Isles

With a foreword by
Jennifer Ogden

HODDER &
STOUGHTON

First published in Great Britain in 1968
by Hodder & Stoughton
An Hachette UK company

This edition published in 2016
by Hodder & Stoughton

1

A CIP catalogue record for this title is available from the
British Library

Hardback ISBN 978 1 473 64124 2
Ebook ISBN 978 1 473 64123 5

Typeset in Plantin Light by Palimpsest Book Production Limited,
Falkirk, Stirlingshire

Printed and bound by CPI Group (UK) Ltd, Croydon, CR0 4YY

Hodder & Stoughton policy is to use papers that are natural,
renewable and recyclable products and made from wood grown
in sustainable forests. The logging and manufacturing processes
are expected to conform to the environmental regulations of the
country of origin.

Hodder & Stoughton Ltd
Carmelite House
50 Victoria Embankment
London EC4Y 0DZ

www.hodder.co.uk

for
ANGELINE and ROBERT,
with love

Dear Reader,

The Wind off the Small Isles is a perfect example of Mary Stewart's perfect writing.

In all of her novels, as with this one, Mary always travelled to where she was going to set her book. Whilst she was there, she would make copious and detailed notes in order that she always had everything in her scenes set correctly. The extraordinary descriptive power of her writing shows this to be the case. Nothing less would have done for her with this novella set on the island of Lanzarote.

Mary spent several holidays in the Canary Islands with her husband Fred, an eminent geologist and professor at Edinburgh University. It was a visit to Lanzarote – some part of which was spent clambering in and out of extinct volcanos! – that inspired this small volume. Fred had decided he needed Mary in his photos so that when he was using them in lectures he would be able to show his students how to gauge the size of the craters. Oh, the things she did for love. But just as much as these adventures, it was the local legends and the numerous and diverse numbers of wildflowers and the rugged, stark topography of this island which inspired her to set her story here. The title is really evocative of what it is like on Lanzarote: wild, beautiful and definitely windy.

As her niece and also her constant companion for the last twelve years of her life, I came to know Mary Stewart (Aunty Mary) extremely well and also to realise how lucky we have been as a family to have had within it this extraordinary and fascinating woman. I miss her terrific sense of humour, her flashes of brilliance, her kind heart and her generosity to everyone she met or knew. Most of all, though, I recall her love for us, her nieces and nephews. We took the place of the children she could never have. The memories of her visits when we were small are filled with scenes of a beautiful woman who always smelled heavenly (Chanel comes to mind now), who was exquisitely dressed and always came armed with presents.

I am sad there will never be another new Mary Stewart book, but the ones she wrote will stand the test of time to be read over and over again by new generations. It is so pleasing that this lovely, lost little book, *The Wind off the Small Isles,* has finally been re-published, in time to celebrate what would have been Mary's one hundredth birthday.
I hope you enjoy reading it.

Jennifer Ogden
23 May 2016

Prelude

She knelt on the window-sill, looking out over the sea. The night was clear, with a faint moon rising, but the stars seemed dim and far away. It must be imagination, but they were not white tonight; the evening star had risen apricot-yellow, and now the main flock of stars crowded hazy and ill-defined above a horizon smoking with purple and cinnamon and grey. This was strange, for the day had been sharp and fine, with a sky settled to blue again after the eruption, and the wind blowing strongly from the north, straight from Cape Finisterre and the coast of Spain and down the chain of the Atlantic islands.

Anxiously she peered into the darkness. Yes, the wind blew still. On the wall of the goat-pen near the cliff's edge she could see the bougainvillaea tossing, and above the roof the palm-leaves shuffled and clicked like playing cards.

Her father had gone to bed long since. He had won tonight, and lying wakeful, waiting, she had heard him call a jovial '*Buenas noches*' after his friends. Then the heavy door had shut, and the men's footsteps, with the quick pattering of old Señor Perez' donkey, had dwindled up the lane into silence.

I

That was two hours since, and soon the moon would rise clear of the cactus slopes behind the house, and by its light she would see him coming.

Mother of God, let him come. He promised, and I know he is true. I know he will come. He promised.

The rosary moved in her fingers, but she was not praying. That time was over. This was now, the night itself, the night the prayers were to be answered. The clenched beads scored her fingers, and she shut her eyes. When she opened them again, he would be here, his boat stealing round the headland into the bay . . . Till then, she would shut her eyes on that empty sea, and think about him, as if by thinking she might make his coming sure.

Against the fizzing dark inside her eyelids she could see him now as she had first seen him three weeks ago, down there on the white sand of the bay, the muscles glancing and sliding under his brown skin as he braced himself in the shallows to pull his boat inshore. She had turned quickly away, as a modest girl should, but Conchita had run, child-like, down to the boat to peer in at the catch of fish. She had hesitated then, and called, but the child paid no attention, and then the young fisherman had turned, straightening, and smiled at her. He was barefooted, and his breeches were ragged, and faded with salt and sun, but the light ran and glinted on wet gold skin and black hair, and she could think of nothing but how the smile drove the deep crease down his cheek and lit the dark eyes . . . Then the smile had gone, and he was staring, and she had stood with her eyes on his and her heart choking her, till Conchita had run back, laughing, and pulled at her hand.

She opened her eyes, and he was here. Round the north headland, shadowy on the shadowy sea, the boat stole like a night-bird, under sail. She thought she could even see him, a shape at the tiller, dark against the sea-fire as the boat heeled in the gentle curve that would bring him into the bay.

She left the sill and moved over to the bed. Her sister's breathing was so quiet that it hardly stirred the air. She hesitated, stooping over the bed, the rosary dangling from her hand, its tiny cross swinging on a silver link. She tugged at this, and the link parted, and she dropped the cross, warm from her skin, on the child's pillow. Then she picked up the bundle of clothes wrapped in her shawl, and paused with a hand on the door. A cloud, thick and dark, drove past the window, but she did not need light to show her the room in whose familiar safety she had slept every night of her eighteen years – the bed of Canary pine, the coffer with its worn oak carving that had been her great-grandmother's dower chest, the wrought-iron candlesticks, the crucifix on the wall: they had been here all her life, they had spelled safety and love. Now she would spell love her own way. And safety, too . . .? Mary Mother, but she must believe what her heart told her, and soon she would be sure . . .

She slipped out through the door and along the flagged passage to the kitchen. The dog raised his head and blinked at her, and his tail thumped briefly. The wind blew strongly, and in the draught the straw mats rose along the flagstones.

Something drove rattling against the window-panes, like a handful of rain. The moon's light had gone, and now she saw how the dark clouds smoked across the stars. Against them, suddenly, light beat redly, and was gone. Then she smelt the faint, familiar reek, and knew the clouds, the sleet, for what they were: the ash-cone to the north, the little Loma, had woken again and was throwing out more ash and cinders. And the wind blew from there.

She checked, while beside her the dog flattened his ears, and his ruff stirred. If she called now to wake them . . . La Loma was harmless; all it had done last week – all it ever did – was to shower the place with ashes, and singe a field or two . . . Ten minutes, and the boat could be clear of the island and beyond pursuit . . . But call them she must. She could not go like this, leaving them asleep . . .

As she turned back from the door, she felt the air move like blast, and round the door the light pulsed red, then died to black again. The dog's chain rattled; he whined, then began to bark, furiously. Somewhere a door slammed, and she heard her father's voice. They were awake. She pulled open the heavy door as the night lit once more with an arched jet of fire, and the smell of blown sulphur rolled over the yard. A gull went up from the roof, screaming, and as she ran past the pens she heard the beasts bleating with fear.

Her father called out again, and she saw her bedroom window flower with light as he ran in with the lamp. Her sister's voice answered, shrill and startled. The light sharpened suddenly as he approached the window. The pane was thrust open, and the light spilled out to catch her where she stood, pinned against the outhouses like a moth.

She saw the big head thrust out, peering past the flame. The night was black again. The mountain held its breath. But he saw her. He shouted, 'It'll be no more than last time. Let them bide, but see the windows are boarded. Then get yourself to the cellar with your sister.'

The casement shut. The lamp withdrew. As she put a hand, dutifully, to the gaps that served the pens for windows, the mountain shot out a plume of fire that lit the night and showed her the boards fast in their places. She turned and ran across the yard and down the cliff path.

He was there. He was waiting for her below the cactus slopes, as he had said he would wait. He had his best suit on, and a cloak made of coarse blanket, and he was bareheaded.

He put his arms out for her and she ran into them.

I

Stolen to this paradise.

KEATS: *The Eve of St Agnes*

My employer, Cora Gresham, is a woman of wealth, and also a woman of whims. She is a writer of children's stories, anything from riproaring adventure to animal cartoons and space fiction, and has the habit of using exotic and authentic backgrounds for what she calls their educational value. In consequence she is liable to set off for the most out-of-the-way corners of the world at a moment's notice, and the life of her secretary and personal assistant − myself − is by no means a dull one.

It came as no surprise, therefore, when it was the turn of a new 'Coralie Gray' adventure about pirates along the Barbary Coast, to be told to get things in train − and that within a matter of days − for a visit to the Canary Islands.

This was my fault, if fault it can be called. I had had to do all the preliminary research; I had combed through loads of books from the library, haunted travel agents and pestered the air lines, and then presented Mrs Gresham with glowing and wildly enthusiastic descriptions of the islands which from time out of mind have been known as the Fortunate Isles or the Isles of the Blessed, and which, we are told, were the original Garden of the Hesperides.

7

And if there weren't still nymphs and golden apples, I told her, there were still dragon trees, and the great Mount Teide, twelve thousand feet high and crowned with snow, and for all we know with Atlas still up there on his shoulders, carrying the sky. There were warm indigo seas lapping on black lava beaches, and aquamarine seas lapping on white beaches, and everywhere flowers and bright birds and perpetual summer . . . I don't think she was even listening. She sat looking at a map of the Canary archipelago, while outside the windows the northern English rain beat solidly down on the brave, soaked daffodils of March. Then she put a finger on the map.

'That one,' she said.

'Lanzarote? But you can't possibly – weren't you even listening? That's the one I told you was practically a desert! It's all volcanic ash, and the book says it's like a lunar landscape or something from another world. Heavens, they filmed *Two Thousand Years before Christ* there, and I'm told it looks like it!' I drew in my breath. 'What's more, there's a great chain of volcanoes called the Fire Mountains, still hot and active, and probably going off at any minute—'

'It's the one nearest Africa,' said Mrs Gresham.

'I dare say it is, but your pirates could just as easily get from the Barbary Coast through to Grand Canary, or Tenerife, and either of those would make a perfectly gorgeous setting.'

'Probably, but I've been looking at the references you gave me, and it seems to have been Lanzarote they usually got to first. Look here at the map and you'll see why. The point is that, apart from all the landings recorded – and there were a good many – there must have been dozens of small raids going on all the time, so anything I like to invent can fit in very well.'

'Yes, but does that actually matter?' I looked over her shoulder. 'There must have been raids on the other islands, and you see how the Barbary Coast lies north of the Canaries, so if your pirates cast just a little further west they'd have missed Lanzarote and the other dry island – what's it called? Fuertaventura – and come on the fertile islands in the westerly group.' I ran my finger down the map. 'That way.'

'I see that, but I think it really will have to be Lanzarote. It fits my story too well.' She tapped the pile of books beside her. 'You remember that I want my pirates to run an expedition to recover some of their friends taken in the slave raids? Well, the Counts of Lanzarote seem to have done a tremendous amount of slaving along the African coast. In fact, I thought I might even use a genuine return raid, the one some time in the 1580s when the Countess of Lanzarote had to hide in that cave under the lava beds. I forget where you put the notes.'

'They're here. Yes, the Cueva De Los Verdes. All right, I give in. It would be rather good, I see that. I'll put it down as a "must" for us to explore.'

'I'm sorry you won't see Teide and your dragon trees,' said Mrs Gresham. 'Some other time, I hope. And I'm sure Lanzarote can't be as bad as you make out. It's even coming on to the tourist route now, isn't it? It wouldn't do that if there wasn't something to be said for it. At least one person I know – James Blair, as it happens, and my younger son was with him – spent a few weeks there getting over the flu last year, and I remember reading something he wrote about it. He loved it. He called it "the last paradise". Of course Michael raved about it, but that's nothing to go by, all he thinks about is swimming.'

'I'm rather that way myself. Ah, well, at least it will be

different. Though as for "paradise" – I suppose it's all in the mind. According to the pictures there are no trees, and they have to make special holes in the volcanic ash to grow their fruit, and there'll be no flowers worth mentioning because it only rains about two days in the year.'

'And that,' said my employer, closing the atlas with a snap, 'settles it. We go there. Fix it up, will you?'

There is one thing about Mrs Gresham, when she has made a decision she sticks by it. Now that she had decided on Lanzarote, she would find it delightful, or die in the attempt. So when precisely ten days after the conversation (in my own way I am as efficient as Coralie Gray) she surveyed the strange, windy landscape of Lanzarote and exclaimed, 'But Perdita, it's beautiful!' I was not surprised. What did surprise me was that I found myself agreeing with her.

The island was every bit as wild and barren as I had imagined. The roads stretched, pitted and dusty, between ridges of black basaltic lava. The only tree was an occasional palm, the only hills the symmetrical cones of dead volcanoes, or, to the south, the great burnt ridges of the Fire Mountains, with the frozen black floods of lava filling the valleys between them. There was no grass. There were no woods. The villages were pure African – square flat-roofed houses painted white and ochre, set flat like little boxes on the baked earth. Above them, where one looked for minarets, the towers of the Spanish churches looked incongruous and foreign.

Strange and exciting, you would have thought, rather than beautiful. 'Paradise' – no, never. But then it got you. You stopped the car on some deserted track they called a road, and got out into the silent afternoon, the thick dust muffling even the sound of your footsteps. You stood looking at the long, yellow fields, with their pattern of growing corn like ribbed velvet, the soot-black slopes honey-combed with pits each enclosing a fig tree in brilliant green bud, the burning range of volcanic mountains shouldering up in great sweeps of red against the dazzling sky . . . all these made a tranquil and somehow intensely satisfying pattern of shape and colour in the pure air. It was beauty more than naked; beauty pared to the bone. And always there was the wind. Cool and steady, the trade wind – 'tracked wind' – funnelled its way down through the small outlying islands to overleap these dry eastern isles and drop its rain on the flowers and green forests of Tenerife and Grand Canary.

It was on our second day in Lanzarote that Mrs Gresham decided that she would buy a house there.

'It really is the perfect retreat,' she told me. '"Paradise" was true enough, if by that you mean something out of this world. Just think of the peace and quiet, think of the sunshine, think of being able to get all the help in the house you want without having to worry about it.'

'Think of being nearly two thousand miles away from home. Think of the Canary telephone system. Think of having your mail all opened and read. Think of not knowing a single word of Spanish except *mañana* and *hasta la vista*,' I said. 'Besides, I'd leave you. You know perfectly well you couldn't do a thing without me. I practically write your books as it is.'

'Dear child, I know. But you'd love it, you really would. It isn't as if it would be for ever, just a year or two—'

'A *year* or two? Now, look—'

'What's a year to you? You can spare it better than I can, after all. No, I'm serious. This might be the place really to pause and take stock of oneself, and maybe write something worth while.'

'Everything you write is worth while,' I said, promptly and firmly. I knew this mood. Mrs Gresham, who is nothing if not clear-sighted, once called herself 'the clown with the normal clown's urge to play Hamlet', but this didn't seem to me to fill the bill. I called it her 'Sullivan act' – a finished master of light music breaking his heart to be Verdi. I said: 'I wish you'd stop tormenting yourself because you're not Graham Greene or James Blair or Robert Bolt or someone. The number of people who'd miss "Coralie Gray" if you stopped writing could be laid end to end—'

'I know, I know. It's all right, you don't need to hold my hand today. That's one reason why I think I would like to stay in this place, even if it's only for a few months – there really is peace here, and yet not a relaxing peace. Tranquillity's the word. One would be hedged in by quiet-ness, and I think one could write. Look over there, nothing but sea and sky and wind and the small islands . . .'

We were sitting – we had been picnicking – on the northernmost point of the island, the Bateria del Rio, where a high cape rears a windy head of red cliff some fifteen hundred feet above the blue slash which is the strait between Lanzarote and the white island of Graciosa. Graciosa is white because it consists entirely of sand, save for the grey cones of its three dead volcanoes. Beyond these ghostly pyramids, more dimly, floated the shapes of the other islands.

'Even their names,' said Mrs Gresham. 'The Pleasing Isle, the Isle of Rejoicing, the Clear Mountain, the Eagle's Rock—'

'You're surely not thinking of living *there*!'

'No, that's a little bit too peaceful, even for me. I'd go round the bend in a week, and what you'd do I hate to think.' She shivered suddenly and pulled her coat round her. 'And the wind. I don't like the wind.'

'Don't you? I love it.'

'You're young. When you're my age you'll find that "the wind on the heath, brother," is only good for rheumatism and damaging the garden. Come back to the car. We'll go home the other way, and see if we can find somewhere sheltered.'

I picked up the picnic things. 'There's always the Cueva De Los Verdes, where your Countess hid out during the raid. Do you want to visit that this afternoon? I think we go right by it.'

We found the signpost – a rather chichi affair of polished rustic work and antique lettering – which pointed the way off into a plain of tumbled black lava, but when we had bumped our way hopefully along the appalling track, the only 'cave' we could find was a large gaping depression in the lava, more like a quarry than a cave. It looked as if the top crust of solidified lava had collapsed, exposing a section of an underground tunnel which ran into darkness under the sharp and overhanging edges of the hole. We looked at it without enthusiasm.

'Well, that's it,' I said. 'Even if you could get in; it simply wouldn't be safe without a guide. What do you say I fix it up and bring you back another day?'

'And that would let you out?' She laughed. 'All right. Go and turn the car while I take a look round the top.'

It was quite a relief to be back on what the maps were pleased to call the main road. Some way further on, right in the middle of the lava plain which stretches along the north-east coast, we saw the notice sticking up: 'Plots for Sale.'

It was about as reasonable as seeing 'Good Building Land' advertised in the middle of the Solway mudflats. This was old lava, from long-ago eruptions, nothing more nor less than a plain of dusty, broken black rock with cutting edges, lightened here and there by the brilliant yellow-green sponges of some succulent, and the phalli of the candelabra cactus, like clustered stands of organ-pipes acid with verdigris. Nothing else grew. As building land it was ludicrous. The only way one could live there was to buy one of the caves that gaped here and there in the lava – monstrous holes disappearing into blackness – and set up house in that.

'Cheaper, too,' I said. 'Look, if you want to use a cave for your story, why don't we just go to the Jameos del Agua? It's another cave near here, and they've turned it into a restaurant, so at least it should be easy to get into. It shouldn't be far away – in fact, isn't that a signpost a bit further along the road, to the left?'

'It looks like it. Well, if you like. Do you suppose they'd run to a cup of tea?'

'I'm sure they would.'

'Then *vamos*,' said my employer.

But the signpost did not mention the Jameos del Agua. It was merely a board, weathered white by sun and the salt wind, on which had been roughly painted the words *Playa Blanca*.

'Doesn't that mean white beach?' asked Mrs Gresham. 'If it's like those lovely beaches in the south there might be a café—'

'I'm sure there won't be. This isn't the tourist end of the island – I mean, you can see why, can't you? And that's not a touristy kind of notice, it's too shabby and genuine. If it leads anywhere at all apart from the beach, it'll just be to a farm or something.'

'Go down, anyway, and let's have a look.'

'I thought you were dying for some tea?'

'There might be something there. In any case, we've still got some wine left over from lunch, haven't we? And if it is a white beach you can have a swim.'

'This being the one day I haven't brought my swimming things.'

'It mightn't matter, at that. Go on, it would be lovely to find a quiet place right out of the wind, and the shore down there's bound to be sheltered. We'll probably find we've got it all to ourselves.'

'I wouldn't be surprised,' I said grimly, as I put the car in gear and turned it off the road into a horrible track that plunged down at right-angles through the lava bed. It was like driving through a coal tip. The black dust was at least six inches deep, and the wheels churned and skidded through it, every now and again jerking across hunks and ruts of broken lava, so sharp that I was in constant terror for my tyres. The track became a lane, deep between lava walls crowned with the candelabra cactus, which after a while gave way to a sort of jungle of prickly pear, so thickly grown that not even a goat could have pushed its way through. We ploughed steeply downwards, trailing our wake of black dust.

'I only hope if we do get down that there's a place to turn,' I said.

'It must go somewhere. After all, there was a signpost.'

'It might only be to a beach. If I've got to turn on sand—'

'You could reverse up.'

'You've got to be joking.' We bucketed round a bend between the monstrous cactus hedges. 'Thank heaven for that! There's a farm or something, there's bound to be a

gate where I can turn. Look, we really will have to stop
here, I'm afraid. I daren't go further. Any minute now one
of these tyres will go phut, and then we really will have
to spend the night in a cave. It isn't far to the sea from
here, we can walk down. I'll manage the picnic things.'

In fact the farm gate, set back to our right, marked the
end of the track. Beyond the gate this dwindled merely to
a path for goats, which wound its way even more steeply
downwards for twenty yards or so, then branched off to
zigzag down the shallow cliff towards the glimpse of white
sand and sea.

I stopped the car between the stone gateposts. 'I'll have
to drive right in to turn. We'd better ask them.'

'Drive in first,' said Mrs Gresham reasonably, 'then they
can't stop you, can they? Besides, you've got to leave the
car somewhere, and they might let you leave it in the yard.'

'You've got a point there.'

Inside the yard was the usual clutter one associates with
a peasant's smallholding – a wood-stack, buckets, what
looked like a galvanised-iron trough. I only vaguely saw
them as I turned the car carefully in between the gateposts
and manœuvred to turn. But beside me I heard Mrs
Gresham make some sort of subdued exclamation, then
she said, sharply for her: 'Look. Just look at that.'

It was certainly very picturesque. The house was single-
storeyed, low and flat-roofed, with a 'picture' window facing
the sea, and a garnet-red bougainvillaea tumbling over a
whitewashed wall. Behind the house was the big beehive
shape of a primitive oven, with the wood stacked beside
it. Between the long front of the house and the edge of
the low cliff there had obviously been at one time a sprawl
of buildings; sheds and sties roughly built of mudbrick
and undressed stone. These now lay tumbled into piles of

rubble. Masonry and wood lay everywhere, and I realised that the trough and the buckets I had noticed were not farm implements at all, but builders' tools, and that there were no animals about, nor any signs of them. Now that I came to look at it, the house itself, with its new whitewash and the modern window, looked too sophisticated to be one of the primitive farmsteads we had seen elsewhere.

I knew what Mrs Gresham was going to say, and she said it. 'My house. This is it. No wonder my Daemon gave me a nudge and told me to come down here. This is my house, Perdita. Look at it. All we'd have to do is knock down the rest of these old sheds in front and floor the yard to make a terrace, and look at the view we'd have. Straight out of that window – the sea, and that flash of white sand at the bottom, and those black cliffs reaching up with their arms holding the bay. And not a living soul.'

'Well, somebody owns it,' I pointed out.

'Indeed yes, and now's as good a time as any to look for them and ask about it. You can do it. No, don't gape at me like that, my child. Switch the engine off and go and knock on the door.'

'Me? Why me?'

'Because I'm fat and fifty, and you're twenty-three and a dish,' said my employer frankly. 'You'll at least get a hearing, where I might not.'

'A hearing? And what do I use for Spanish?'

'Anything you like. If they're Spanish all you have to do is smile at them and they'd listen even if you talked Gobbledegook.'

'Well, thanks, but—'

'Now stop arguing, and go and see who lives there. They might speak a bit of English anyway, and at the very least you can probably find the name of the owners. Then when we get back to Arrecife we can make enquiries, and get a lawyer to take over from there. Go on, I'll wait in the car.'

I got out resignedly, and picked my way across the yard to the door, which was set deep in an archway in the end wall of the house. It was a thick, studded affair of heavy planking, which had recently been given a lick of blue paint. If it had been any use arguing with my employer, I would have pointed out that the new paint, and the evidence of building operations, suggested that someone had recently moved in and was doing on his own account just the improvements she had suggested, but I knew from experience that Mrs Gresham's impulses had to be allowed to wear themselves out in their own time, so I merely lifted a hand and knocked at the door.

The wood must have been very thick. The sound seemed to drown, almost, in the door itself. No echo. It was like knocking on a solid wall instead of a hollow door.

I waited for a bit, then tried again. Still no answer. But when I turned away, half in relief, Mrs Gresham called from the car:

'I can hear something round the other side. Someone talking, I think. Go round the front, I think they're at the far end.' And she waved towards a grove of palm trees and some softer green which showed beyond the house.

I went. At least it would be shady, and it was pleasant to be out of the car. It was mid-afternoon now, and the sun was hot, but a small breeze wandered even here, clicking the leaves of the palm trees. These made a grove of shade where a small patio had been newly laid out at the far end of the house and out of sight of the entrance yard. The patio, facing the sea, was enclosed on its three landward sides by the wall of the house, by the slope of black lava which rose steeply behind the house and was formidably overgrown with prickly pear, and by a black wall – now grey with builders' dust – where a gap made a gateway to the cliff top. In the shade of the palms stood a white painted metal table with a chair drawn up to it, and two or three brightly coloured beach chairs.

There was no one there. But a portable typewriter stood on the table with a pile of paper beside it weighted down by a rose-coloured shell. On the top page I could see a line of typing which looked like a title: *The Wind Off The Small Isles.*

'Señorita?'

A man's voice, sharp. I jumped and turned.

He was standing in the gap which opened on the cliff top. I hadn't heard or seen him coming, and now I saw why. Beyond the wall a small clump of tamarisk trees waved their frothy green at the cliff's edge, and in their light shade two men lay dozing, hats tipped over their eyes. Beside them was the remains of their meal, and a little further off some shovels, buckets and piles of what looked like sand and lime. They seemed to have been building a kind of low retaining wall along the edge of the cliff. It was their voices which Mrs Gresham must have heard, and now I had interrupted their siesta.

The man who had spoken was evidently some kind of foreman, for where the other two wore patched and dirty khaki trousers and the floppy straw island hats, and apparently worked stripped to the waist, this man had on a pair of reasonably decent blue denims and a short-sleeved shirt open at the neck. He was bareheaded.

'Perdóneme,' I said. 'Buenas tardes, Señor.'

'"*Tardes*.' He was unsmiling, but this didn't mean

anything. Spain is not, like Italy, a land of flashing teeth and ready hands. He waited for me to explain myself.

'*Por favor, Señor*—' But here my Spanish ran out. At the sound of my voice the other two had roused themselves, and were sitting up, staring. I tried the smile that Mrs Gresham had recommended. 'Excuse me, but do you speak English?'

'Yes.' I thought there was something wary about the admission, as if he wasn't quite sure what it was going to let him in for. He was much younger than the other two. 'Can I help you?'

'It's only – my friend and I were driving down from El Rio and we saw the signpost and came down this little road to see what there was, and she . . . well, we couldn't turn the car, so we drove into the yard. I hope you don't mind?'

'Not at all. You wish me to turn it for you?'

'Oh, I can manage, thanks. It isn't that. My friend . . . as a matter of fact she's my employer . . . she sent me to ask what this house was and who owned it. I did knock at the door, but no one answered. I suppose it's a bad time to choose, siesta time? I'm sorry if I'm intruding.'

'There is no one at home.' He said no more, just waited there in the gap of the wall. If I was to find out anything at all I was going to have to persist. Perhaps he hadn't understood my rapid English. I spoke more slowly:

'Then perhaps you would just tell me – is the house itself called Playa Blanca, or is that the name of the beach?'

'It's the name of the beach, but the house goes by that name too. It's the only one here.'

The sun was making me blink. I moved a pace into shadow, narrowing my eyes at him. 'Surely you're English?' His eyes were hazel, not dark as I had thought. 'Is it your house, then?'

'No.'

I am not by nature aggressive and persistent, but since these are qualities which Cora Gresham values in her secretary, I persisted. 'But you speak it so well, *Señor* . . . Now I won't interrupt you any more, but I wonder if you'd just give me the name of the owner, please? That's really what my employer sent me to ask.'

I thought he hesitated. The other two men were on their feet now, staring at us, and he gestured irritably to them with some phrase in Spanish and a glance at his watch. As they trudged off to their buckets and cement, he turned back to me. 'I'm afraid I don't know. I only work here.' There was in fact, I noticed now, a faintly discernible Spanish accent. 'We are employed by an agent in Arrecife. Now we turn your car, eh?'

He crossed the patio, and with a gesture invited me to precede him back to the car. We walked together along the house-front.

'An agent in Arrecife?' I said. 'Then if you would be kind enough to give me his name? Just for the record, you know.'

'*Qué?*'

I stopped dead and turned. A hoopoe, startled, shot off a ruinous pigsty with a flare of camellia-rose and brilliant barred wings. Beyond it the sea flashed and glittered. The silence was profound.

I faced him squarely. 'Look, I'm sorry, but it's as much as my job's worth to let you push me right out without getting some kind of answer. And don't pretend you don't understand what I'm saying, because your Spanish accent's only just descended on you like Elijah's mantle. You are English, aren't you? And you've probably only just moved in, which is what it looks like, and you don't want to be bothered answering a lot of questions from someone who's obviously interested in the property? Fair enough, you wouldn't dream of selling – then all you have to do is say so. But wouldn't it be just as easy to tell me the name of your lawyer in Arrecife and let him do it for you? Straight up, it's as much as my job's worth to go back to the car now and tell my employer I haven't found out a thing about it. What's more, it's the quickest way of bringing her down on your neck that I've ever known. Just give me chapter and verse, and I'll clear us both straight out of your life and never come back.'

He grinned. It made him seem all at once much younger. 'That'd be a bit rough when I've only just met you, but if you want the truth, it's as much as *my* job's worth to tell you.'

No trace of Spanish accent now. I regarded him curiously. 'Top secret stuff? You mean you've actually had instructions not to tell?'

'Yes.'

'I'm right, they have just bought it? English?'

'Yes.'

'Well, that lets us both out, doesn't it? Relations of yours, parents?'

'No. I'm just assistant, looker-upper, apprentice, architect, watchdog, chauffeur and quite often keeper. But I'll tell you this, there isn't a chance in a million that my employer would dream of selling. This is his idea of the perfect hideout. I'm supposed to guard the gate like Cerberus and stop everyone coming in except the girl who brings the milk. Hence the strongarm stuff, for which I apologise, but orders is orders.' He waved a hand to the emptiness in front of us. 'He sounds like a wanted criminal, but he's not. All he wants is peace, and he thinks he's found it here.'

'Then this is where I came in. That's what my employer says, too, and what's more, your job sounds very much the same as mine – p.a., chauffeur, dog, devil and dairy-maid, and whatever you call the person who is sent out in front to draw the fire. As now.' I turned away. 'All right, if you've had your orders, this is something she will understand. They're two of a kind.'

'Mine's a writer,' he said apologetically, 'and more or less mad north-north-west.'

'I was busy guessing that. So's mine. That's what I meant. I don't mean she's mad – I must admit she's perfectly sane – but I see what you mean for all that.' I paused. 'Well, I'm sorry to have bothered you. Don't come any further, or you'll have to turn Spanish again. I can manage the car quite easily. Goodbye.'

'Half a minute, don't go yet – look, it's not my fault I've had to clam up like this, so won't you make it good for evil and tell me your name? Where are you staying? The hotel in Arrecife?'

'Yes. But I reckon I don't owe you my name.'

'Have a heart, I'll tell you mine. It's Mike, short for Michael—'

'Michael!'

We both jumped and spun round. Mrs Gresham was standing at the corner of the house, and as we both gaped at her, she screeched again: 'Michael!'

'For crying out loud.' There was more surprise than ecstasy in the young man's voice, but he advanced to meet her, and submitted cheerfully as she folded him to her.

Over her head he grinned at me. 'Well, what do you know? It's Mum. No wonder you said your employer needed a keeper.'

Mrs Gresham released him. '*Did* she?'

'Actually, she didn't. That was me.'

'If there's one straitjacket I covet more than another,' said Mrs Gresham, 'it's James Blair's. Perdita, as you'll have gathered, this is my son Michael.'

'I – is it? I mean, yes, we've met. I was just getting my breath back. So it's James Blair who lives here? I'm afraid he's beaten you to it, Mrs Gresham. He's just bought the house, and he's not parting.'

'You've seen him?'

'I have not. Your son said he was out, though I have no means of knowing whether that was the truth, but when you happened along I was being thrown out neck and crop, if that's the right expression, and you were to go too, but if he's your son he can't very well now, can he?'

'Certainly not. He's going to entertain us to tea,' said my employer, leading the way smartly towards the chairs under the palm-trees.

2

Ay, ages long ago
These lovers fled away . . .

KEATS: *The Eve of St Agnes*

'Well, now, Mike,' said Mrs Gresham, settling herself comfortably, 'what's all this about? I thought you were in Morocco.'

'Oh, we were. But ever since we stayed here before – in Lanzarote, I mean, the time he had flu and wanted to recoup so that he could finish *Tiger Tiger* for Julian Gale – he's talked about getting a place here as a bolt-hole.'

'I know. He told me about it.'

'Well, he'd asked an agent in Arrecife to keep his eyes open and report if anything suitable became vacant, and a couple of months ago it did. So here we are, moving in.'

It was coming straight now. The younger of Mrs Gresham's two sons had ambitions himself to be a playwright, and a year or two ago had, so to speak, apprenticed himself as research assistant and jack-of-all-trades to James Blair, one of our leading playwrights and a friend of the family. I had gathered from Michael's mother that learning, rather than earning, was the object of the job, and from the rare letters she had received it seemed that her son was enjoying himself hugely, the periods of gruelling work no less than the fallow intervals of travel and study. '*Michael was with him at the time, and raved about the swimming . . .*' That was probably the letter she had had at Christmas, written from Morocco, and I knew there hadn't been one since. Well, since I gathered that James Blair worked his assistant as hard as Cora Gresham worked me, Michael Gresham wouldn't write letters unless he had to. Few men did. Nor had he been home since I had been with his mother, so I had never met him, but now that I came to look at him, I could recognise through the dust and dishevelment the Mike Gresham of the younger photograph which stood in his mother's study; dark-brown hair, hazel eyes, a face that would have been undistinguished except for its shrewdness and humour and (what the photograph didn't show) the attractive crease that his sudden smile drove down his cheek.

He was smiling now. 'Look, do you really want tea? Won't you make it wine? It'll come up good and cold from the cellars. We're right over a nice holey hunk of lava here, and we've a genuine *cave*. Yes?'

He vanished into the house, from which he presently emerged carrying a tray with glasses, ice, olives and a bottle of the pale local wine called Chimidas. He set these down on the table, moving the papers on to a chair to make room.

'I know one's not allowed to notice something that's only half done,' I said, 'but is that his? Another play?'

'We hope so.' He began to pour the drinks. 'Only in the thinking stage as yet, and snag-ridden as usual. Ice? Try some soda, it sounds disgusting, but it makes a long cold drink with a mild sparkle, very refreshing when you're hot. There. Like it?'

I accepted the long misty glass, and sipped. 'Mm – yes, it's rather good.'

'My own invention.' Then he turned to his mother, and the two of them plunged into a rapid exchange of news, from which I gathered that Michael liked the job very much, and that he didn't expect the Canary Islands phase to outlast the writing of the play. 'Though goodness knows how long that will be. He's been going through a bad period, a more or less complete block since he got *Tiger Tiger* off his desk. If it's been anything like as trying for him as it has been for me—' He grimaced. 'Still, we may be through it now. Down in the forest something stirs. He's prowling round and round a new theme, so here's hoping.' He raised his glass, drank, and smiled at me. 'Do you go through this with my mother?'

I shook my head. 'Didn't you know? When she's stuck I just write them for her.'

'These rarefied agonies are not for me, thank heaven,' said Mrs Gresham. 'So he plans to stay here till it's finished? That could be a long time. What about you?'

'Oh, that's what he says,' said Michael, 'but you know what he's like, restless as the devil, and uses up about as much energy in a day as keeps most people going for a week. We'll no sooner get the place straight than he'll be fretting for London again. Not that I'm grumbling. I'm all for change myself, and let's face it, there are certain obvious lacks in this paradise of his. Or were . . . Well, Mother, it's your turn. What on earth brings you to Lanzarote?'

'Pirates,' said his mother concisely.

'Not Barbary Bill again? I thought you killed him off at the end of *Coast of the Corsairs*.'

'Dear boy, I can't afford to kill off my best-selling buccaneer. Reports of his death were found to be much exaggerated.' She set down her empty glass. 'No, no more, thank you. It was delightful. Now, Perdita and I are staying at the hotel in Arrecife, so the next time you can get off the chain, come and have dinner. Now we'll go. I don't want James to come back and find us here; I know how I feel about being interrupted myself. Give him my regards and tell him he'd be welcome, too, if he feels like an evening out.'

'For goodness' sake, don't go, he won't mind *you*,' said Michael. 'Some interruptions he minds, and some he doesn't. I mean it; do stay. I know he'll be pleased to see you, and you might think of me, marooned here all this time with only the workmen and my revered employer for company! In any case, work's over for the day . . . His, that is. Mine goes on.' He gestured, not to the typewriter, but to the workmen busy along the cliff.

'Good heavens,' said his mother, apparently seeing them for the first time. 'What are you doing over there?'

'Saving money and labour. As we demolish the goat-pens or whatever they are, we carry the stones along and use them for the retaining wall.'

'Will it be safe? It's very near the edge.'

'It's safe enough where the house is, never fear. I'm not so sure about the sides of the bay, but this centre part is solid. We're taking the retaining wall a little way along there to the right . . . Over that way there are one or two cracks in the surface lava, but they only go a short way down, and later eruptions obligingly filled them up with volcanic ash.'

'I see,' said his mother drily. 'I was wondering what you'd been doing to your clothes. He interprets "assistant" pretty liberally.'

Michael laughed. 'I enjoy it.'

'That I can see. You surely haven't done the alterations to the house yourself?'

'Oh, no, a real builder made the window, and rebuilt the main fireplace and made the kitchen usable, then he looked at the rest of the job and sold us his advice and the materials. Actually it looks as if we're doing an awful lot, but all that we've done ourselves is pull down the outhouses. They were just about derelict anyway. The builder comes and takes a look at us now and again, and his lads know their stuff . . . Everyone on this island seems to know all there is to know about working with stone. Have you seen the way they terrace the slopes?'

He had turned to me with the question, but before I could reply he looked quickly past me towards the house.

'What is it?' asked his mother.

I knew already. While he had been speaking I had heard the sound of a car bucketing down the horrible little lane. Now a door slammed, rapid footsteps crossed the yard, and James Blair came round the corner of the house.

I knew him from his photographs, of course. One's first impression of the famous playwright was that he looked very like Beethoven. He was a smallish man with deep-set eyes, a wild bush of hair, and a quiet manner which seemed to hide immense reserves of nervous energy. His voice was deep and rather harsh, and he occasionally hung on a word in a way that suggested a stammer overcome. It was only after some time that you realised he was shy.

He stopped dead when he saw us. Michael got to his feet. Mrs Gresham said:

'Well, James!'

James Blair's face changed. 'Cora Gresham! Well, well . . .' He came forward and met her outstretched hand. His look of pleasure was obviously genuine. 'Looking Mike up? He gave me away, then?'

'Not a word. It's pure accident that we came across

him, believe it or not. This is one of those coincidences that nobody would believe if you or I put it into print – at least, if you did they'd say it was a subtle denial of causality, and if I did they'd say it was romantic nonsense . . . James, this is Perdita West, who writes all my books and protects me from the world, presumably as Mike does for you.'

We murmured greetings, and shook hands. Mike said, grinning: 'Let's hope she's a bit more efficient at it than I am, letting my mother loose on you like this. I'm sorry, James.'

'From what I know of your mother, whom I esteem dearly,' said Mr Blair, 'Miss West's job will mainly consist of protecting the world from her, not her from the world. Isn't that so?'

I laughed, shaking my head. 'I want to keep my job.'

'I'll get you a glass,' said Mike. He picked up the typewriter and papers to leave the fourth chair vacant for his employer, then vanished with them into the house.

His mother glanced after him. 'I'm told we may be going to have a new play from you?'

'It may come to something. At present it's quite hideously in embryo, all beginning and no end.' He pulled one of the chairs forward and sat down between us. 'But at least it *has* a beginning. I was on the verge of deciding I'd dried for good. You know how it is? For the last few years I've been lucky, one thing so to speak begetting the next as I worked, but after *Tiger Tiger* the vein ran out.' He spread a broad hand on his knee, regarded it for a moment, then looked up at Mrs Gresham with simplicity. 'It never happened before, and it frightened me to death.'

'It was probably just the flu.' Her tone was not unsympathetic, merely matter-of-fact, and it must have touched some common chord of understanding, because he laughed, relaxing back in his chair and stretching his legs in front of him.

'Probably. If so, it wasn't such an ill wind for me after all – it blew me to Lanzarote to recuperate, and so found me this house, and my story.'

'How do you mean?'

He turned the hand, palm up. 'The story belongs here. Actually here, to this house. Something that happened here.'

'Then you've robbed me twice over,' said Mrs Gresham.

'Robbed you?'

'Certainly. That's why we're here. I'd no idea this was your house, or that my son was here. Perdita and I simply came down to look at the beach, found we couldn't go any further, and drove into your yard to turn. Thereupon I fell in love with the house and sent her along to find out who owned it, and if there was anything to be done about buying it. She ran across Michael, who was un-cooperative, and would have got rid of her in double-quick time if it hadn't turned out that I was his long-lost mother. So you see you have robbed me, first of the house, which I envy you bitterly, and now apparently of a story, too. If I had only got here first I would have fallen heir to both.'

He laughed. 'I'm very sorry.'

'Well, there's a divinity that shapes our ends. No doubt the story, whatever it is, will come off rather better as the new James Blair than as the latest adventure of Sockeye the Salmon or the Teenage Pirates. Those,' added my employer modestly, 'are two of the world-beaters I am currently engaged with. I can't expect you to know.'

'I was brought up on Beatrix Potter,' said Mr Blair, 'and if I were forty years younger I'd be an ardent fan of Sockeye the Salmon.'

'Aren't you nice? I suppose we're not allowed to know this story? I'm afraid I couldn't help seeing the title, but don't worry, silent as the grave, and of course Perdita is, too. At least tell us where it comes from? I thought the "small isles" were the Hebrides?'

'Not this time.' This from Mike, coming out of the house with a glass and another bottle. 'It's just a phrase we used translating from the Spanish.' He spoke a phrase in that language. 'That just literally means the wind from the little islands – in this case the islands off the north cape, Allegranza, Graciosa and the rest. If you've been that way you've probably seen them. James?'

'Thank you.' Mr Blair took the glass. 'Yes, I suppose the phrase "the small isles" suggested itself because it was familiar, though heaven help us, we might be on a different planet here.' He sipped the wine absently, both hands cupping the cool glass, his gaze slowly travelling over the green bubbles of cactus, the black basalt, the glittering sea, the cloudless blue, focussed seemingly not on them or beyond them but on some sharp point of light thrown by them inward into himself, as by a burning-glass. But his voice was ordinary, even faintly apologetic. 'The story . . . As a matter of fact, it's hardly a story at all, and what there is of it is so ordinary, so much the classic cliché of a love story, that told baldly like this it hardly bears repeating. But there's something there, if one could find the treatment.'

We all sat watching him. I thought to myself, there's always something there, if one can find the treatment. The same old material, the same old line, the same old setting – all that counts is the quality of the mind that processes them. And this was the man – I looked up suddenly and caught Mike Gresham watching me. His eyes flickered and he looked away quickly.

'And I can't even pretend there was anything exciting or dramatic about the way I found the material,' James Blair was saying. 'I suppose you'd gather that this used to be a small farm. It was a rather specialised kind of farm, Lanzarote style . . . As you can see, there's nothing in the way of arable, or grazing for anything except goats. It was a cochineal farm.'

'A cochineal farm?' I exclaimed.

He smiled. 'It sounds ridiculous, doesn't it? About as ridiculous as a silk-worm farm, only a cochineal farm is far less picturesque. You see those great slopes of prickly pear behind the house? That doesn't just grow there by chance, it's been deliberately planted, because it's the host to the insect from which you get cochineal. It used to be one of the main industries of Lanzarote, but with the introduction of aniline dyes the bottom dropped out of the cochineal market, and the farms which relied simply on the one product went out of business, this one among them. There's a limit to what can be done with land of this type. This has been nothing but what you might call a small run-down steading now for years, so when the last owner died the farm was put up for sale – very cheaply. The owner was the last of the family who'd lived at Playa Blanca for a couple of hundred years, and the place was sold just as it stood, furniture and all. There was nothing of any particular value, but it's real Canary Islands stuff and it suits the place and I find it attractive.'

'And then,' said Mrs Gresham, 'in the secret compartment of the old deck you found the papers?'

He laughed. 'As I said, it's all in the treatment. I did find papers, certainly, but highly unromantic ones. Simply a shelf of files, and two or three books of farm records – accounts, mostly, and on the whole not particularly interesting. Mike had a look at them – his Spanish is fairly good – but they turned out to be just a sort of log, giving details of crops, harvests, prices and so on. Well, that might have been that, except that I've never been the kind of person who could sit idly in an interesting place and not begin to think about it. It occurred to me to wonder if there were anything interesting recorded about any of the eruptions, for instance. The last big one was in 1824, and I had an idea the logs went back that far at least, so Mike and I got the books out and started hunting.'

'And you found?' I asked.

'Very little – but this in itself is interesting, wouldn't you say?'

'How?'

He turned up a hand. 'I take it you've seen the Fire Mountains in the south, and those appalling deserts and glaciers of lava? Most of it was thrown up in the eruptions of the 1730s, which went on at intervals for about six years, and devastated hundreds of square miles; then part of the same area was destroyed again in 1824. Well, there's no reference to the eruptions in the log book except to say that "Cousin Andrès from Yaiza came over with his daughter and his dromedary". He seems to have stayed, and ten years later the daughter married the son of the house. The inference one draws is that Cousin Andrès lost his house and land – and possibly the rest of his family – in the eruptions.' He looked at me. 'But it remains an inference. That's what I find interesting, humanly speaking.'

'I see. They take eruptions in their stride here.'

'Shall we say they give them rather less news-value than we give a snowstorm at home?'

'And Cousin Andrès from Yaiza gives you your story?' asked Mrs Gresham.

'No, no. A ten years' love affair is hardly dramatic material, would you say?'

'I wouldn't, certainly, but then Coralie Gray's readers like love at first sight, however much cynics like you and my son may deny it ever happens.'

'Did I?' said Mike.

'Almost certainly,' said his mother. 'It's the kind of thing young men do deny, isn't it?'

'I can see I'd better guard my real story from you with my life,' said James Blair, 'because it is love at first sight, and it would probably suit Coralie Gray down to the ground.' He hesitated. 'You'd really like to hear the rest? I'm afraid the bones are very bare as yet, but you know as well as I do, Cora, how it goes.'

I saw her smile, and knew why, but I don't think he noticed. He was moving off again into his private world. As I watched him I became conscious – as one is of a switched-on heater – of some other steadily focussing concentration. But when I glanced again at Michael, he was studying a grasshopper on the pavement beside his foot.

'After that first entry,' said James Blair, 'we read the rest of them for the time of the eruptions. Did I say that the 1824 eruptions lasted about three months? The only other reference to them was that "the wind off the small isles by God's mercy blew day and night, and carried the smoke and ash away to the south, thus sparing this end of the island."' He paused. 'That was Mike's translation. It struck me at the time. I told you the other thing that struck me – the almost routine acceptance of this kind of cataclysm. I went back through the books to see if there was the same kind of reaction, or lack of it, to local eruptions here in the north. I knew that the main eruptions at this end of the island – the ones which made the dead cinder-cones and the old lava fields that you drove through today – those eruptions would be a good deal earlier than 1824, but of course in any volcanic island there are small disturbances from time to time which may not have even been recorded, I mean at a national level. Mike and I hunted through the books to see if any of them had happened here.'

'And had they?'

'Yes, once or twice in a small way. But what caught our eyes was the same phrase again, used this time in an entry about an eruption just north of here. Is there any more wine, Mike?'

'Sure.' Mike refilled the glasses.

I said: 'If the eruption was to the north, and the "wind off the small isles" was blowing again, I suppose it would bring the gas and ashes this way?'

'Certainly it would, but, true to form, that's not what the entry was about. Something was going on here in the house on the night of the eruption that affected the writer, the farmer, a great deal more than any local volcano going off. His daughter eloped.'

'Ah,' said Cora Gresham.

'I told you this would be up your street. Her name was Maria Dolores; she was the elder daughter, and there was a fair amount of money; at that time the cochineal farm was still doing well. His name was Miguel, and he was a boy from a poor family in Mala, who used to fish from the beach down below there, the Playa Blanca. It seems nobody knew anything about it until it suddenly happened. It seems doubtful, even, if the boy and girl had exchanged more than a few words. You may be sure that at this date – it was 1879 – even if Maria Dolores didn't have an official duenna, she would be well looked after. But it seems they just looked at one another and fell in love. As girls did in those days, she'd collected over the years a good dowry, clothes, household goods – you know the kind of thing – but none of it was touched; her younger sister got it all. All Dolores took with her that night was a small bundle of clothing, and her silver rosary. All the boy owned was his boat, and as far as the elopement was concerned, it was enough.'

He took a mouthful of wine. In the hot silence I could hear the small, clear ringing of a bell, as the goats strayed grazing along the cliff. From where I sat I could see three of them moving nearer in Indian file, up a path that scored a shallow diagonal across the face of the southern arm of the bay. They ambled, white and yellow-dappled, past the black gape of a crevice in the angle of the cliff, then leapt one after one over the rock beyond the retaining wall to pause, grazing apparently with relish, among the cochineal cactus.

'And that,' said James Blair, 'is all we know. She left a note for her father, but we're not told what was in it. "*Ages long ago These lovers fled away into the storm.*" Did I tell you it was St Agnes' Eve, January 20th? Only this time it wasn't the frost-wind blowing, "*pattering the sharp sleet Against the window-panes,*" it was the wind from the small isles, full of smoke and hot ash and gases. But it was, all the same, the right wind for them. They took the boat from Playa Blanca – at any rate it vanished and was never traced – and the wind would take them straight to Fuertaventura and the other islands. And in 1879, even Grand Canary was far enough away.'

'The father never tried to trace her?'

He shook his head. 'She's never mentioned again, and her younger sister fell heir to everything she should have had. Dolores is written off then and there. "Let her not return. The wind from the north still blows, and it is all she shall inherit."'

There was a short silence. Then Cora Gresham asked: 'How are you going to finish it?'

'I don't know yet. I'm still looking for the point of entry. I see it as the father's story, rather than the lovers'. I said she had been written straight off, but that wasn't strictly true. There was one other entry, made a week or so later, but not mentioning her name. It just said, "The rosary was the one I bought her in Las Palmas, of silver with each bead made like the leaf of the cochineal pear. Very pretty." Here, Mike.' He thrust his glass at Michael, and stood up abruptly. 'Now, come and see what I'm doing to your dream house, Cora.'

'Delighted to.' She got up and followed him to the edge of the patio. 'Good heavens, what's that?'

She was staring out to sea, apparently at something beyond the north arm of the bay. I stood up to see, then stared in my turn. A short way out, previously hidden from us by a jut of the cliff below, floated the ghost of a ship. Literally a ghost. It was an old fore-and-aft schooner, its warped timbers bleached to silver, which rode quietly above its grey reflection in the shelter of the curved coast. No canvas, no rope, no sign of life. A ghost ship from years ago.

'It can't be true,' I said, still staring.

'It's true enough,' said Mike from behind me. 'It's an old ship somebody in Arrecife bought a little while ago, and they've moored it down here. Weird, isn't it? It's just a shell, quite empty. I'm told the idea is to make a night club or a floating restaurant, or something of that sort. We were scared stiff they'd improve our horrible little road, and bring all the cars down this way, but there's a better track further along and they're going to use that.'

'Well, James,' said Mrs Gresham briskly, 'that's *my* story, at any rate! I take it you don't want the copyright on that? No? It's exactly what I want for my pirate story. Maybe it's not exactly the right kind of ship, but since I've never been on an old sailing ship at all, this will do marvellously. Is there any chance of getting across and looking over it?'

'I don't see why not. Mike can fix it for you, if you like. In fact we've got a boat in the bay; we can take you across ourselves, once you've got permission. Now come along, and I'll show you the house.'

As I turned to follow them Mike touched my arm. 'Will she want you to explore the ship with her and take notes, slave-girl, or could you come swimming with me?'

'Won't Mr Blair want you to row the boat, slave-boy?'

'Probably. We could leave them there and come back. Perdita—'

'Yes?'

He appeared to review, at speed, some half-dozen statements, reject them all in turn, and come back to banality with a kind of relief. 'Do you do any skin-diving?'

'Love it. Is it good here?'

'Terrific. Sandy bottom, and submerged reefs and outcrops from the cliff, and plenty of small caves where the sand runs in and there's lots of weeds and fish. Sheltered, too, so the water's usually clear. You'll come?'

'I'd love to.'

'Then let's go and put the screws on your employer,' said her son, 'and get them to make it soon, shall we?'

3

. . . Like a mermaid in sea-weed,
Pensive awhile she dreams awake . . .

KEATS: *The Eve of St Agnes*

In the event, I went without him. That evening when
Mrs Gresham mentioned the old ship in conversation with
the manager of our hotel, it turned out that the next day,
Sunday, would be the only reasonable chance she would
have of seeing over it until the following weekend. He
knew the new owner very well, he told us (a cousin of my
wife, you understand?) and he would himself telephone
immediately and seek permission. There would be no difficulty, no difficulty at all . . . Naturally, the Señora was at
liberty to go any day of the week, but she must understand
that there were men coming on Monday to assess its possibilities as a floating restaurant, and they would be coming
and going all week. So if what the Señora wanted was to
gather atmosphere, to try and visualise the ship as it had
once been . . .?

This was certainly what the Señora wanted. We set off
next morning.

Since the farm at Playa Blanca was not on the telephone,
we had not been able to warn James Blair of our prompt
return. And when for the second time our hired Volkswagen

bumped and slithered down the abominable lane the farm seemed as quiet and deserted as it had yesterday. In fact more deserted. There were no workmen there on the cliff below the cactus slope. When my knock failed to get an answer I walked right along to where the piles of sand and cement lay covered with tarpaulins against the dew. No sign of life but a family of rosy-looking bullfinches flirting and twittering over the tamarisks.

'Not a sign,' I reported to my employer. 'Sunday, of course. And the car's gone, too. What do you bet they're all at church?'

Mrs Gresham snorted. 'The day George St Bernard Shakespeare darkens the door of a church I'll eat my royalty cheque,' she said. 'Never mind, let's go down to the bay. They're probably down there swimming.'

'Their car's gone,' I repeated.

'We'll go down anyway.' She got out of the car with decision. 'There's no point in staying here. The only thing I'm afraid of is that they'll have taken the boat away and gone fishing.'

For myself, I rather hoped they had. I had horrible visions of having to row my employer out myself to the schooner. But I said nothing, just picked up my swimming things and the picnic basket and followed her down the path.

They weren't in the bay, but apart from that, luck was in for both of us. The boat – a boat – was there, and beside it at the water's edge a boy, a young man of about seventeen, stood with bare feet in the creaming shallows doing something to a fishing line.

He spoke a little English, and he and Mrs Gresham very soon came to terms. He would certainly row her out to the schooner, he said, and she could stay there as long as she liked. He would be within reach, fishing. She had only to call him, and he would come and bring her back. And the Señorita . . .?

My employer looked at me. 'Do you want to come?'

'Do I have a choice?'

'It's your day off, Sunday, remember?'

'So it is. Well, do you need me to take notes or anything, or would you feel better with someone else there?'

'No to both. All right, my dear, enjoy yourself. And don't start watching the path yet. Church doesn't come out for at least an hour.'

The boat was afloat and half out through the white breakers, before I could think of anything to say.

The water was cool, and alive with chill, stinging bubbles. I sat on a flat rock and put on my mask and flippers. The sea was tranquil, its long, shallow swells lifting and falling softly like a sleeper breathing, but since I was alone and didn't know the shore I had no intention of diving, but decided to cruise along the reefs at the surface or just below it. I adjusted my mask, gripped the mouthpiece of the snorkel in my teeth, and lowered myself into the water.

Anyone who has ever done skin-diving will tell you that there is one moment they will never forget – the first time they ever put on the mask and looked down at the bed of the sea. It is, literally, like opening a gate on a new world. And for myself the first few moments of every dive bring the rapture of discovery over again.

And this was new country. The colours and shapes, the life and tempo of this ocean bed were as different from the sea-beds I knew in the North Sea and the Mediterranean, as the Mountains of Fire were different from the Cotswold Hills.

I saw no sea-anemones, no starfish or urchins or grey

coralweed, none of the thick bladdery straps or green sea-mosses of our home water, just the clean sand, unrippled, the sharply shaped rocks, and the drifting patterns of the thin clear weed. Weeds in sable and silver and olive moved like windblown hair, like cloud, like waves themselves across a sea-bed of every shade from gold to grey and white, with the ripples of shadow and reflection pulsing across it as the sea moved. A school of tiny white fish drifted below me, a score of them all moving together like tiny paper fish on some mobile stirred by a current of air. Then all at once, twitched by some invisible master-thread, they slipped to the right and were gone. A pair of striped fish nosed across at right angles, then hung motionless a foot above their own shadows. Something emerald-green and vivid shuttled ahead of me, from shadow to light to shadow again.

I surfaced, and reached with my feet for the sandy bottom. I was not much more than breast deep. I must have been cruising with the drift of some current, for I found that I had swum – as one always does – further than I had imagined. I had gone right along one arm of the bay, and was standing now almost below the southern headland. I couldn't see the farmhouse, set back as it was from the centre of the bay's crescent, but the tops of the palm-trees were visible above the ruined outbuildings. Beyond the other arm of the bay the bleached hulk brooded over its glimmering reflection. Though I could see no sign of life aboard her my employer must be there still, as the fishing boat was a little way beyond the ship, the boy busy in the stern over net or line.

I looked up at the towering black basalt above me. The skirts of the cliff thrust out into the sea in ridges or folds, as the lava had spilled, almost like stiff pleats of black

43

velvet, forming a series of narrow coves or inlets. In cruising along the base of the cliff I had found myself passing from light to dark and back to light again, as these buttresses threw and then withdrew their shade. A little way out to sea the water whitened round black stacks of rock, some of them massive enough to act as breakwaters, so that the water along the foot of the cliff was calm.

I turned, and began to trudge back the way I had come.

I idled along the surface, the sun warm on my skin through the milky water. There was no sound but the *hush* of the far waves, and the occasional booming echo of the swell as some tongue licked into the caves and smoothed creaming under the hollow rocks. Spray hissed and whispered, and my whole body and mind were brimful of that happiness and well-being which sunlight and salt water and peace can bring.

I don't know whether it was the same emerald fish I had seen before, or one like him, but this time I came full on him at a distance of about two feet as I rounded one of the lava buttresses into a pool where the sunlight struck full on the golden floor of the sea. It was hard to say which was the more startled, the fish or I. We both stopped short, back-pedalling, staring at one another, I with delight, and the fish with no expression that I could read; there was almost certainly no delight, but there was no fear, either. He hung there just ahead of me, green and gold and kingfisher-blue in the clear water, for a full ten seconds before he jack-knifed away into the shadow of the cliff.

To this day I can't be sure if it was just reflection from the brilliant sea-bed, or if he really did switch his lights on as he went into the darkness, but I saw him flash away under the buttress, trailing light like tracer fire. I moved in to get a closer look, swimming down from the sunlit

44

pool into the black inkwell of shadow under the cliff. For half a minute or so I had him still – a moving glimmer of green in water black as squid's ink, then I lost him. As I trod water, searching, my feet found sand and I surfaced once more, to find that I had swum right in under the cliff, and was standing at the back of a shallow cave, looking out under a low arch at the bright distant prospect of the other side of the bay.

The water came up to my armpits, and the roof of the cave was barely two feet above my head. The air was warm enough, but it smelt oozy, and in contrast to the brilliant light outside the place was gloomy and full of echoing gaps of blackness and the horrible sense of the impending weight of the cliff above. I don't like caves. Besides, the outer arch of this one barely cleared the surface of the water, and would be filled by any kind of swell. I preferred to look at the sea-bed, where motes of sunlight dropped towards me through the bright ellipse. I put my head down and pushed off in a shallow dive towards the light and the open air.

Or rather, flexed my knees to push off. I was barely afloat when something, some enormous disturbance of the water, surging into that cave like blast, drove me back off my feet and clean off balance and pitched me with a shock-wave of noise and violence and bellowing water, right up against the roof of the cave.

I must have been knocked unconscious for a few seconds. All I remember is the sudden shock, turmoil, and then blackness. My head must have struck the roof of the cave, but the mask and snorkel had taken the worst of the blow, and though I later found bruising and grazes on my back and shoulders, the chill of the water had deadened the skin, and now I felt no pain. With the breaking of the tube of course my mask had filled with water, and I suppose that, half-conscious as I was, all my instinct and sense were concentrated on the struggle to get out of the mask and into the air before I drowned. The same instinct kept me afloat, but here without any effort of mine the sea helped me. When at length I tore my mask off, gulping for air, I found I was high and dry on what seemed to be a narrow shelf of sand and shingle running steeply up against slimed and pitted rock.

I say 'seemed to be'. Because now I could see nothing. I clung to the rock, feeling the tug and suck of the sea and the pebbles which grated away from under me, pushed the soaking hair back out of my eyes and, gasping and retching for breath, tried to fight off the feeling of un-believing nightmare. The cave-mouth had disappeared. Where there had been a slit of brilliance doubled by its reflection, there was now nothing but pitch-black night and storming water and this appalling, booming echo that slammed through and through my brain and body as though I were some blind polyp lodged helpless in the roaring spiral of a shell.

But even when the tossing of the sea had smoothed a little and the echoes begun to abate, and sense came back and with it balance, the steadying of my world brought me no comfort. I realised now what had happened. A section of the cliff had slipped from above, and falling into the shallows, had set up the shock-wave that had mercifully thrown me back on to the dry inner shore of the cave. But at the same time it had sealed me in. Of the cave-mouth, the light, the outer world, there was no sign.

4

In sort of wakeful swoon, perplex'd she lay . . .
Blinded alike from sunshine and from rain.

KEATS: *The Eve of St Agnes*

It is impossible to describe the confusion of the next few minutes, or even to remember how long I crouched, bewildered and terrified, sightlessly clinging to my rock, while the water swung and dragged at me, and with its movement the trapped air under the shallow roof beat like blast against the eardrums.

But at length the tumult subsided. The water sank to an intermittent swell and heaving, and the terrible noise no longer rocked the air. My throat and eyes burned with salt, and I felt limp from the hammering I had received, but at last I was able to loose my panic hold of the rock, and think.

I had almost written 'look about me for a way out'. This, in fact, was what I found myself doing, eyes wide on the dead darkness, staring from side to side as if the very concentration of my looking could conjure up some glimmer of light to show me the way. But no light showed. The darkness was complete.

I do not want to remember, much less describe, the waves of panic that beat at me periodically during all this time, much as the sea was beating. I think the worst of it was not being able to see. I knew there was air to breathe, and even the trapped air under the shallow roof felt fresh, as if there were an outlet somewhere, but claustrophobia is beyond reason, and though I told myself that Cora Gresham and the fisherman knew where I had gone, and must have seen the fall of rock, I could not sit still with the dark closing round me, and wait for them to start searching; I had to find a way out.

The first thing would obviously be to reconnoitre the mouth of the cave, but of course I now had no idea in which direction this lay. The only guess I could make was that the inrushing swell would have washed me towards the back of the cave where, in the brief glimpse I had had before the extinguisher dropped, I thought I had seen a steep narrow beach which could be the one where I now sat. I convinced myself that if I slithered straight into the water at right angles to the rock, and swam carefully forward, I should be swimming towards the new fall of stone across the cave-mouth. It was even possible, I told myself, that if some big block of the cliff, breaking off cleanly, had fallen down across the opening, there might be space underneath it through which a diver could go; and there might, as the turbulence cleared, be some glimmer of light which could be seen under water to show me the way.

The snorkel had disappeared, but I still had my mask, and this seemed to be undamaged. I put it on, lowered myself into the water and, with my hands out in front of me to protect my head, swam slowly forward.

It is not a pleasant experience, diving in darkness, when one may be diving against rock. And rock was all I found. It was not far down to the bottom, and I kept myself down there as long as I could, and as still as I could, straining my eyes through the glass in every direction. Once, some moving creature brushed my bare arm, and I had to exert every scrap of self-control I had not to gasp myself full of water, and jack-knife to the surface or up against whatever rock overhung me. It was only my emerald fish, I told myself – only the fish; and I held myself down, groping along the sand, the rock, staring blindly round me into blackness.

The trivial incident was enough, in these circumstances, to shake me badly. The moment I had convinced myself that there was nothing to be seen, no possible safe way out, I surfaced, about-turned, and floated myself cautiously back towards my beach.

And even the simple right-about-turn proved to be impossible. I miscalculated. Where my outstretched hand should have met sand and shingle, it met rock, and at the same moment my knee jarred and grounded on a subterranean ledge, and some belated swell washed me once again hard against the wall of the cave.

Luckily here the wall was as smooth as licked toffee, but the shock and unexpectedness of it threw me off balance, so that, forgetting the dangerous lowness of the roof, I grabbed for the nearest bit of wall, found a hand-hold, and heaved myself out of the water to kneel upright on the ledge.

And stayed upright, safely anchored to the slippery rock. There was plenty of headroom here. I don't know how many seconds it took me to grasp the fact that my hand-hold was a smooth metal ring embedded in the rock.

I explored it with my fingers. It was big and heavy, and obviously corroded with age. It was like one of those enormous handles you find on cathedral doors, or the rings to which you moor a boat. And you don't moor a boat – I thought, with sudden excitement – anywhere where you can't step out of it . . . Whoever had driven that ring into the rock must have stepped out on the ledge where I now knelt. This was flat and smooth, with a right-angled rise behind it just like a step . . .

It was a step, just above water level, hewn out of rock – as my questing fingers told me -- but smooth and flat, and lifting in its turn to another rise, and another step . . .

I suppose if I had stopped to think it would have occurred to me that this might merely be a landing stage for boats using the cave in some long-past time for storage or shelter, but I wasn't reasoning. To the blind creature that I was, crawling about the bottom of the black well, steps led upwards, steps led somewhere out of the trap, into air and light . . .

I stripped my mask off, then, with my right hand clamped tightly on the ring, and my left arm bent above me to protect my head, slowly let myself stand upright. There was room. Above my head my hand met nothing. I straightened the arm, stretched it – nothing. I felt carefully forward with a foot. Another step . . . and another . . .

I let go the anchoring ring, and carefully, using hands and feet, began to edge my way up the steps. Four, five, six . . . and my left hand met rock, and the stairs shrank V-shaped as the staircase bent right-handed. I clambered on, all the time protecting my head.

I did not stop to wonder where the steps could possibly be going, or what purpose they could ever have served; I just blindly dragged myself up this miraculous escape from darkness towards the upper air.

And the air was fresher here. There was even a slight warmth, a reminder of sunlight not too far away.

And at last, light.

Not so much light as a faint slackening of the darkness, the promise of a gleam round some upper curve of the stairway; but it had all the collision and glory of the first light on the first day of creation. You would have thought it was a floodlight shining right down the stairs and illuminating every step. I straightened my body, dropped my hands, and ran up towards the glimmer as if the rough steps were a well-lit staircase at home, and at the top was a landing and a lighted door.

There was indeed a landing, of a sort. The steps gave on what seemed to be another cave, and the light was here, filtering somehow indirectly but effectively enough through cracks in the roof and right-hand wall – the wall which should be the outer shell of the cliff. Because the rock was black basalt it drowned, instead of reflecting, the light, but at least I could grope forward without flinching, and where there were small cracks open to the light, there might be bigger ones.

The wall to my left – immediately beside me as I emerged from the stairway – showed lighter than the rest; it even had some faint colour about it, a sort of ghost of burnt umber; and as I put a hand to it to feel my way forward I felt a different texture, crumbly, ash rather than basalt. As my hand patted and groped along it trickles of dampish ash dislodged and fell with a whisper. Behind me, like an echo, came another whisper, another fall. I stood still, my heart hammering. I was remembering what Mike had told me about the cracks in the lava crust on this side of the bay, and how the later eruptions had filled them with ash. There had been ash on the steps, I remembered; and in the swirling pool below I had been bombarded with gritty particles too heavy for sand. There must have been a fall of ash into the sea when the rock came down. Surely I hadn't climbed this miraculous stairway of escape just to find myself at the source of the avalanche?

Another fistful of the russet ash broke away just beside me, smoking down to spatter over my ankles. I moved cautiously clear, trying not to cough, and bent to smooth the sharp stuff from my bare feet. Something caught my eye, something that the fall had uncovered, a pale-coloured object lodged in the hollow the falling ash had left. It was greyish-white, and the light caught it clearly. A hand, stiffly protruding from the wall. A hand and arm, draped in a grey fold of cloth from which the ash still scaled with a pattering like small sleet.

Even the darkness had been better than this. I seem to remember standing there for quite a long time with my eyes shut, telling myself first of all that my senses had lied, that this could not possibly be a hand, and at the same time insisting – shouting to myself – that the hand was dead, and that dead hands and dead bodies do no harm . . .

I would have to look at it. Presumably when I got out of this prison (my brain shied from the word *tomb*) I would have to tell someone about it. I opened my eyes, and looked again.

It was still there, and still unmistakably a hand, but now almost immediately something about its colour and the disposal of the drapery along it brought a doubt, and with the doubt, relief.

The arm, now exposed to some way above the elbow by the constant steady crumbling of ash, was curved as if holding some large object, and from this graceful and protective-seeming curve the drapery fell in folds like the cloak of a statue. That this was what it must be I now saw. The greyish-white colour, the stony texture of flesh and drapery alike . . . It was, after all, only a statue.

Only? Under the circumstances I wasn't prepared to get excited about the possibilities of a 'discovery' – but I had to be sure. I reached forward and touched the cloak. My relieved guess had been right . . . It was stone or plaster. I left it and turned again to my quest for a way out.

It has taken a long time to tell this, but from my first moment of startled fear to the moment when I touched the arm and turned away, not more than three or four minutes can have gone by. All the time I had been conscious of the continual crumbling and falling and pattering of the ash near me. Now before I had taken three steps there was a soft, swishing rush and thud, and another section broke from the wall and mushroomed softly up from the floor at my feet.

With it fell something that went with a small dry rattle. I caught a glimpse of some white, stick-like object. A fragment – perhaps a finger? – had broken from the stone hand. The thing was probably rotten with time and damp and stress . . . it was probably slipping, and the mass of compressed ash with it . . .

I fled to the other side of the cave, feeling my way along the rough and mercifully solid basalt, with a wary eye on the rotten wall of ash. Half the statue was exposed now. It was life-sized, the arm curved to cradle something, the shoulder forward, the head bent . . . And it was certainly moving. It wavered and stirred in the now rapidly growing light.

Two seconds later, perhaps, it got through to me that it wasn't the statue that was moving; it was the light. That whatever natural light had led me up to this level had been supplemented for the last half minute by the light of a torch, held in a living hand. And that the owner of the hand was now picking his careful way down from somewhere above and ahead of me, the torchlight welling in front of him through the confines of the cave.

5

And listen'd to her breathing . . .
Which when he heard, that minute did he bless,
And breathed himself.

KEATS: *The Eve of St Agnes*

It had to be Mike, of course.

Not only had it occurred to me that I must have climbed
some way towards the inner curve of the bay and the
environs of the farm, which was the only building here-
abouts, and which must have at some time been connected
with the steps and the landing stage, but also, somehow,
his coming was inevitable. After the first jump and jerk of
my heart when I saw the moving light, I simply stood
there and waited for him. I suppose I had been knocked
half silly, and then badly frightened, and so was for the
time being as entirely self-centred as anyone can be; at
any rate I assumed, absurdly enough, that he was coming
to look for me, sent (miraculously, I suppose, for there
had been no time) by his mother. I leaned against the wall
and waited for him quietly, all fear stilled.

What I didn't reckon on was the fright I would give
him. The sound he made was something between a gasp
and a yelp, then his breath went in more smoothly and he
said with commendable mildness, 'Good gracious me.'

I took a step. I was surprised to find how weak my knees felt. 'Mike. Oh – *Mike!*'

'Perdita! For heaven's sake! How in the world did you get down here?'

'I – I didn't get down. I came up. You – you did come *down*? There really is a way out up there?'

'Yes, of course I came down. We'd just got back to the house when the fall took place, and—' I heard his breath catch again as it got through to him what I had been saying. 'You said you came *up*?' The torch raked me. He said sharply: 'You were swimming? . . . You mean you came up *from the sea*? What's happened? Surely that was Mother I saw on the old ship?'

'Yes. A fisherman took her over. I didn't go with her. I was swimming, and I was in a cave down there, about halfway along the side of the bay, and there was a fall outside, and I was shut in. I – I found some steps, and started to climb—'

I broke off. Suddenly reaction and cold, together, got through to me and I began to shiver uncontrollably. 'I – I'm sorry. I got a bit of a knock when the backwash hit the cave, and then it was pitch dark and I thought I wasn't going to be able to get out—'

He took two quick steps and pulled me into his arms and held me tightly. 'Here, love, pack it in, you're all right now. We'll be out of here in two shakes.'

'Sh – shakes is the word . . . I'm sorry. I'm all right really . . . Oh, Mike, you're sure we can get out?'

'Of course we can. It's not far. Do you realise you're just about under our cactus field?' He talked on, holding me close, deliberately soothing. Warmth seemed to come out of him in waves. 'I told you we'd just got back, James and I . . . we'd been to Teguise to watch some Sunday procession he wanted to see . . . and we heard the landslip. We knew you were here, of course – saw your car in the yard – but then I saw Mother over on the schooner, and the boat just rowing back to it, so I assumed you were there, too. And the ship was obviously OK, but . . .' He paused for a moment. 'Well . . . I noticed that the slip had opened up that crevice under the cactus – you saw the one? I wanted to see how safe it was, so I came down by the goat path. I . . . I happened to have brought a torch, so when I found a lava tunnel had been opened up, that someone seemed to have used some time back . . . Well, it looked solid enough, so I went in to have a look at it.'

'But to come right down!'

He said quickly: 'I heard something moving about, and I thought one of the goats might have wandered in and got caught.'

'A goat? But Mike, you might have been trapped yourself! It could have been—'

'Yes, but it wasn't. Now we'd better get back up as quickly as we can, if you're better?'

'Yes, thanks. Sorry, I was just cold.'

'Good grief, so you are, you're frozen, and no wonder. You'd better have my jacket – here, hold the torch.'

He pushed it into my hand while he took off his jacket. 'There, put that on. Bare feet, too? You poor kid, this lava rock's damned sharp – yes, I thought so, your feet are bleeding.'

'I don't feel them. No, honestly I don't, they're too cold. Leave it, Mike, we'd better hurry. Some of the ash was slipping over there—'

But he had already kicked off his shoes, and was pulling his socks off. 'Never mind that, put these on or you'll tear your feet to pieces climbing out. My shoes are no good to you, but the socks'll help. Here.' He pushed them into my hands, and started putting his shoes back on. 'I'll take the torch now – good God!' He had caught sight of what showed in the moving beam. 'For pity's sake, what's that?'

'It's a statue,' I said. 'I saw it when the ash began to scale away.'

'Good Lord, so it is.' The beam seemed to focus and intensify as he approached the thing. He sounded pleased and mildly excited. 'Do you suppose we've discovered something valuable? How in the world did anything like that get here?'

'Maybe this was used as a storeroom. Or to hide things away during the war, or something.' I was struggling to get the second sock on, brushing the damp, sharp grit from my foot. 'That would mean it was valuable, I suppose.'

'You wouldn't store works of art in caverns on a volcanic island, one would think,' he said. 'Hm, very odd. What sort of stone, I wonder?'

'Mike, watch it, I wouldn't touch, that ash is falling all the time.' I dragged the sock on, and stood up. 'The thing's falling to bits anyway. Let's get out of here, shall we? Look, a piece fell off, we can take that with us and show anyone who's interested, and they can jolly well come themselves and prod round in this horrible cave.' I snatched up the fallen fragment of white. 'This is it, I think it's a finger—'

I stopped dead. The torchlight flicked from the wall to my face, and then down to my hand. I didn't need the light to show me what I held. It was the small bone of a human finger.

I dropped it. In the same moment, as if the downward flick of white had been a hand on the plunger, the wall came down. This time it was a big fall. It came rushing down towards us in a swishing, choking avalanche. In the flying seconds before the torch was knocked from Mike's hand and extinguished I saw the rest of the grey stone-like figure show momentarily, like a ghost against darkness. It was not one figure, but two. In the curve of that shielding arm some smaller body was huddled. I saw merely the double hump of two heads, one bent over the other, the curve of the protecting shoulder, the hand, grey and stony, ending in the delicate, brittle bones – then Mike had whirled with his back to the fall, and dragged me under him with my head pulled down against his chest, and his body arched over mine to keep off the falling ash. The torch went out.

It seemed ages before either of us dared to move. We huddled, clinging together, half buried, half choked by the clogging, shifting ash. Fortunately this was dampish, or we might have been choked in earnest; as it was, the stuff weighed heavily, shifting and pressing closer with every movement, scoring the skin and tearing like a sandstorm at the membranes of mouth and throat as one tried to breathe.

Crouching, my mouth and nose buried in Mike's shirt just above his suddenly thumping heart, I heard, with infinite relief, his little choking sneeze, and felt the cautious movement of head and shoulder above me.

'Perdita?' A hoarse whisper right at my ear.

I licked my lips. 'I'm all right. You?'

'Still alive.' He cleared his throat. 'God, that's better. It's stopped, I'm pretty sure. Hold still a minute, love, till we see what's what . . . I don't want to start this lot moving again by trying to get out too quickly. It won't be difficult, don't worry.'

'Can you see? Has it blocked the way out?'

'No, it's blocked the way you came up, as far as I can make out. Yes, I can see a little . . . I'm afraid the torch has gone, but there's enough light to get out by . . . Can you get your hands over your mouth and eyes? I don't want this stuff pouring in when I lift away from you.'

'Yes.' My hands had been spread against his chest, clinging there. I moved them cautiously in, cupping them against my face. The grit was horrible, and hurt, but I could breathe.

'Right?' His heart had slowed almost to normal now. His voice was comfortingly ordinary.

'Right.'

'Hang on then, I'll try it out.'

It was not as easy as he had made out. We were fairly tightly entangled together inside our cocoon of ash, which had engulfed us to the shoulder-blades: or rather, it had engulfed Mike, who hung over me, his body covering mine as a bird covers its young. Slowly, and with great caution, he began to lift himself off me, pushing the weight of the ash back with his shoulders a little at a time, then waiting for the displaced ash to pour into the gap before he moved again. It was, I imagine, like pulling oneself out of a quicksand, with the added difficulty that he dared not make any sudden or strong movement for fear of starting another perilous slip, or of course of engulfing me. But at last he managed to shoe-horn himself free of the ash, then, kneeling, reached his arms round me from behind, and with infinite caution began to pull me out.

It was the same crushingly slow process. With every movement the ash shifted and poured into the gaps, gripping with its abrasive weight. But I came slowly free, to the waist, to the hips, to the knees – and then with a run that sent Mike staggering backwards, still holding me, so that the pair of us rolled together clear across the floor to collapse in a hard-breathing tangle against the outer wall.

The fact that neither of us made any move to free ourselves this time was – naturally – only because we were exhausted . . . And – naturally – when I turned back into his arms I put my own round him and pulled him to me tightly. His heart had started to thud again, and this time it showed no signs of slowing down. Naturally not . . .

He said, 'We must be crazy.' Then, 'Are you warm enough now?' And later, 'You taste of salt and ashes. Lot's wife or something.'

'At least make it Eurydice.'

'And still in the underworld, my poor darling.' He let me go. 'For goodness' sake, we'd better get out of here! I don't know what we were thinking about!'

'No?'

'Oh, well . . .' he said, and gave me a hand up into the upper passageway.

At the top of the rough tunnel the sunlight waited beyond the crack in the cliff face. Mike put an arm round me and half lifted me through into the golden day.

For a minute or two I could only stand there, dazzled by the light, holding on to him and taking in great gulps of the clear beautiful air.

He shaded his eyes, looking down.

'There's Mother, look, just getting out of the boat. He's beached it. She must have been half out of her mind. They'll have been rowing along the foot of the cliff to see if they could see a sign of you.'

He let out a yell, and waved. Mrs Gresham looked up, and saw us above her on the cliff. Even at that distance, I thought I could detect a wild relief in her gestures as she waved back.

'It's a mercy she can't see what you look like, she'd go straight into orbit,' remarked Mike.

'My lover,' I said warmly. 'Though come to think of it,
I must look at least as awful as you, which is saying a lot.'

He laughed. 'Making love in the dark has its points,
wouldn't you say? My poor darling, do those scratches
hurt?'

'Now you come to mention it, they're stinging like mad.
I feel as if I'd been through several beds of nettles.'

'They'll sting worse when you get under the shower.
Let's go and do that very thing, shall we? Look, Mother's
got your clothes, she'll bring them up. I suppose I'll have
to let you have the shower first, but I warn you, if you
take more than five minutes I shall come in.'

'Make it six, I've got to wash my hair. Mike—'

'Yes?'

'I haven't said thank you for . . . looking after me the
way you did.'

'Nonsense, you'd have got out all right by yourself.'

'I – I might not have. I might have been stuck down
there for ages, perhaps for ever. I could have been buried
alive, just the same as—'

I stopped. The air rustled in some blue flowers close
by my hand. A pair of goldfinches, bright as butterflies,
flew wrangling sweetly into some grey shrub with yellow
flowers.

Mike's eyes met mine. They were sombre. Then he
laughed. 'Worse than death? Don't relax for a minute, love,
that's still to come. But first, that shower. Six minutes,
mind, and not one second longer.'

6

The sculptured dead.

KEATS: *The Eve of St Agnes*

'But it could be, quite easily!' Mrs Gresham was excited. 'What you've found is a Guanche necropolis-cave . . . Perdita, don't you remember reading about them? Yes—' this to Mike – 'the primitive Canary people, before the Spaniards came, they mummified their dead. I think it's the only place it was ever done, apart from Egypt and Peru. They used to preserve the bodies with spices and various plants and the sap of the dragon tree, then they dried them in the sun, and wrapped them in goatskins and put them into caves. Since there aren't any proper caves in Lanzarote, they'd have to use the holes in the lava.' She looked from Michael to me. 'What do you say?'

We were all in the patio. Mike and I had showered and tended our bruises and emerged in turn to meet Mrs Gresham's transports of relief and James Blair's solicitude, which latter included a command to stay and share the Sunday cold duck and salad; so we had duly relaxed with big tulip-glasses of sherry in the shade of the palms, while Mike and I told our stories.

'What do you say?'

I shook my head. 'They weren't mummies. That wasn't

goatskin, it was like plaster or – or some kind of composition. I don't understand—'

'But the finger-bone? You're sure it was a real finger-bone?'

'Quite sure.' I looked up from my glass to find Mr Blair's eyes on me. As if he had spoken, I answered him. 'But it looked like stone, and it felt like it, too. How could it have happened like that?'

'Have you ever been to Pompeii?'

'Why, yes, but—'

I saw Mike look across at him, sharply. 'So that's it? You think it's possible?'

'It's all I can think of. Listen.' He picked up a book, and glanced at me. 'Mike gave me a quick sketch of your story while you were still in the shower, so I looked this out. It's from the *Proceedings of the Society of Antiquaries of London, 1863*, and it's an account of the excavations at Pompeii, and it tells you how they made the casts of those bodies you can see in the museum.' He began to read: '"The ashes in which the bodies were buried must have fallen in a damp state, and hardened gradually by the lapse of time, and as the soft parts of the bodies decayed and shrank a hollow was formed between the bodies and the crust of soil. This formed the cavity into which the plaster was poured. In the bony parts, the space left void being very small, the coat of plaster is proportionately thin, and many portions of the extremities and crania are left exposed. So intimately did these ashes penetrate, and so thoroughly has the cast been taken that the texture of the under garments, drawers, and a sort of inner vest with sleeves is distinctly visible . . ."' He looked up. 'It goes on to say that the folds of the dresses were quite distinct and the bones of the feet protruding.' He shut the book. 'So if they

were caught by the gas, and then the ashes buried them
– well, compared with the two thousand years of the
Pompeii corpses, ninety years is nothing.'

'And the cement I've been pouring down the lava cracks
had the same effect as the plaster at Pompeii?'

'It seems so.'

There was a short silence. 'Poor children,' said Mrs
Gresham, 'they didn't get far, that night. Yes, I'm with you
now, James. Are you going to tell anyone?'

'I shall have to, I think. I suppose they should have
Christian burial, and then we have to see that the place is
safe. The lower cave is almost certainly completely shut,
and the fall that nearly caught Mike and Perdita must have
sealed off the lower stair.'

'When I think of it . . .' My employer drew in her breath.
'She might never have been able to drag herself out of
that alone. Thank God you went down, Michael! Of all
the marvellous chances! There you are, James, that's how
it happens – pure chance, luck, "denial of causality"—'

'Denial of causality be damned,' said James Blair crudely.
'He told me he was going down the cliff to find Perdita,
and where the hell was the torch? I said that Perdita was
over in the ship, and what did he need a torch for in the
middle of the afternoon? I won't tell you exactly what he
said to that because it was – well, abusive, but what it
boiled down to was would I kindly shut up and stop wasting
time and where the sweet so-and-so was the such-and-such
torch, because he thought the old lava tunnel had opened
up and he had a feeling—'

'I always thought it must be a lava tunnel.' Michael spoke
smoothly, and only a little more loudly than usual. 'Most
interesting, geologically speaking. If you've never seen lava
stalactites, James, you should go down before we close it up.'

'What's a lava tunnel?' said I.

James Blair looked from Michael to me, and back to Michael. Then he cleared his throat. 'Very well. I should hate it to be said of me that I couldn't take direction. A lava tunnel, Perdita, is a natural hollow in a flow of molten lava. The surface crust of the lava cools by its contact with the air, and the under-layer on contact with the earth, and these layers insulate the core, so that it stays molten and goes on flowing after the outer crusts have stopped. When the supply of lava eventually ceases, the molten core empties itself – in this case into the sea – leaving a kind of hollow tunnel. That side of the bay seems to have been one such flow. And then later, with cooling and weathering, the thin upper surface – the roof of your tunnel – might crack and leave fissures which could be filled by the next eruptions of gas and ashes. Did you see the Cueva De Los Verdes, Cora?'

'Yes. Just a hole in the lava field.'

'That was the roof of a lava tunnel which had fallen in. This might eventually do the same. If the farm records went back far enough we'd probably find that the cave and the tunnel became a "smugglers' way", and the steps and landing stage were made. Or perhaps there never was a record, and Miguel had found the way by chance, as Perdita did, from the sea. It doesn't seem to have occurred to Dolores' father to look for them there.'

'"The wind from the north still blows, and it is all she shall inherit,"' said Mrs Gresham. 'Poor girl. Would it be quick?'

He hesitated. 'I think we can assume it. The people in Pompeii weren't buried alive, they were killed by the gases, and from the description, that might be what happened here. The concentration of ashes and gas must vary with the lie of the land, so the farm might tend to get off lightly while the main wind overleaped it and dropped the stuff along the headland. You might say it was the wind from the north that killed our young lovers. Oh, yes, it would be quick. A few moments of intense fear, that would be all. Merciful enough.'

I thought to myself: *Not even that. I know how she felt, and she wasn't afraid. She hadn't got further than hearing the beating of his heart, so close, and yet suddenly so sure. Never even alone together before, not properly, and, yet so sure, so sure, that it didn't matter whether 'for ever' meant life's long slow span, or only the next few quiet seconds . . .*

Mrs Gresham mistook my silence. She said quickly; 'Of course we may all be quite wrong – this is probably no such thing as we're thinking. We're obsessed with James' story, so we've rather jumped to conclusions. It wasn't the lovers at all.'

'Oh, yes, it was,' I said.

'What is it, darling?' asked Michael gently. I saw his mother glance quickly at him, but she said nothing.

'This.' I unclasped my hand and held it out to him. 'I found it in your jacket pocket, when I was cleaning the ash out. It must have fallen in when we were buried there.'

'A chain?' He picked it off my palm. It was something like a necklace, only shorter, of metal, corroded and blackened. But you could see from the scratches that it was silver, and that each bead had been made like a leaf of the cochineal pear.

Envoi

And they are gone.

KEATS: *The Eve of St Agnes*

A kestrel swept across the bay, below eye level, the sun glinting rosy on its back. The air in the patio was still and hot, but a wind had sprung up, and above us the palm-leaves shuffled and clicked like playing cards.

'So that,' said Mrs Gresham, putting down her glass, 'really is the end of the story.'

'Not quite,' said Michael, smiling at me.

His mother raised her brows, and this time she did open her mouth to say something, but James Blair shot up from his chair with a sudden exclamation that startled us all. 'No, by God! Look there!'

It was over in a moment, so quickly that none of us could swear afterwards exactly what we saw.

Near the edge of the cliff and a short way beyond the crevice, a grove of cactus plants tilted, slid and vanished. Where they had been, a black hole gaped. Then the cliff's edge slid downwards and outwards in a cloud of dust and ash, and for a moment, no more, the side of the cave-in was exposed.

Then the wind blew in and tore the ash away in a great plume of russet-grey, and hazily through this, for the fraction of a second, we saw them there, Miguel and Dolores, her head on his heart, his body covering hers as a bird covers its young. Then the white shape fell to nothing, and vanished along the north wind into the open sky.

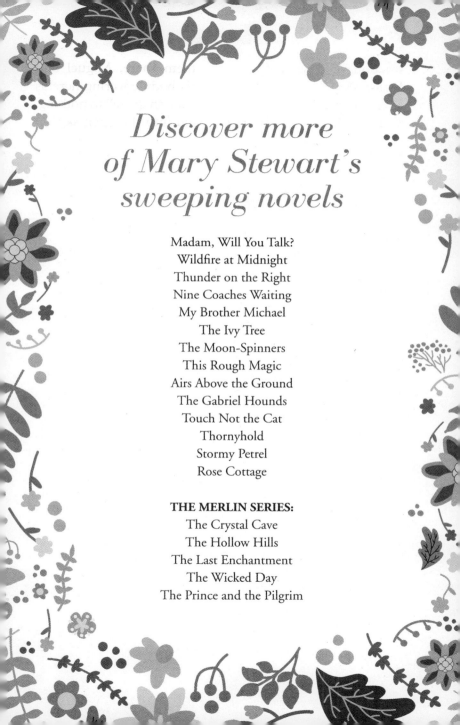

Discover more
of Mary Stewart's
sweeping novels

Madam, Will You Talk?
Wildfire at Midnight
Thunder on the Right
Nine Coaches Waiting
My Brother Michael
The Ivy Tree
The Moon-Spinners
This Rough Magic
Airs Above the Ground
The Gabriel Hounds
Touch Not the Cat
Thornyhold
Stormy Petrel
Rose Cottage

THE MERLIN SERIES:
The Crystal Cave
The Hollow Hills
The Last Enchantment
The Wicked Day
The Prince and the Pilgrim